Brave New Chord

Eve Zennarrow

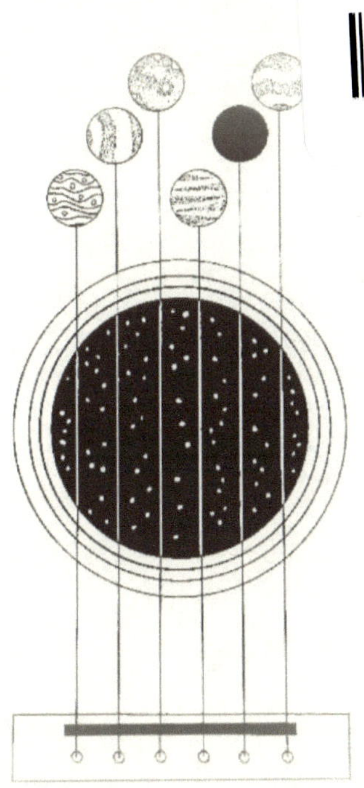

Disarticulated Press

First Disarticulated Press paperback edition December 2025

Disarticulated Press

disarticulatedpress.com

Zennarrow, Eve

Brave New Chord

ISBN 9781764327060 (pbk)

The Mixtape

The following poetry collection was born from a lifetime of listening to music, from decades spent tracing the shape of sound and the ache in a chord. It captures the way a melody can slip into your bloodstream and become a secret part of you.

That's why it's recommended not to read these poems in silence, but with a companion frequency — a shadow of notes to lean into as you read.

Each poem is twinned with a song. Plug in, press play, and read with the sound on:

QR CODE

Brave New Chord

Tonight, I wanted to unfold the sphere of your soma,
inspect the surface of that famous profile,
and try to understand
the constant civil war between your frown and your
smile.

The perfect drug on your skin tastes like geometry.
You're a Rubik's Cube and I want to break you down
until only the core remains.

"Why don't you come over here?" you said.
"Come closer.
Let's dance to Jeff Buckley
while the moonbeams are
sniping through our bare feet."

Your words pierced through me,
an X-ray through soft tissue
and got me dreaming in slow motion:
once the patterns
filled with what other people needed of us
evaporate, and we
overanalyze our error logs,
we could stay up all night
fashioning hopes from the fragmented
beauty others threw away.

You could be my bedtime reminder,
the greatest of all expectations —

inevitably my "off the record,"
and my sound waves on fire.
And I, I could be a harmony
to your dissonance.
Change all your notes for me!
I could be your **Brave New Chord**.

The world will drown in the
never-ending, exultant opus
of my sonder words and your velvet voice.

As we dance, dance, dance
on the water,
weightless and free,
because we chose each other
like we didn't have a choice.
Like I'm a ball and you're a catch,
and we are a perfect match.

"Hug me till you drug me, honey;
kiss me till I'm in a coma,"
you whispered —
and I never felt more understood.

*The quoted line "Hug me till you drug me, honey; kiss me till
I'm in a coma." is from Aldous Huxley's* **Brave New World**
(1932).

(Soundtrack: Jeff Buckley - Lover, You Should've Come Over)
♪♪♪

Entropy in (re)verse

I hugged the emptiest jukebox
with the verse arms of a beginner.
I wanted to hold those lyrics close,
bury them under my ribcage, but—

I have all work and no play fingers
that snap with the rhythm of your blinks.
I can't sell you this bag of nails;
you could hurt your feet on your way out.

I keep painting over a Monet's flowers.
How come there are no cigarette burns
on any of the legendary paintings?

There's something wrong with me.
My thoughts are made of songs
you can't hear on the radio.

I'll send you a playlist in chronological order:
from the most bizarre to those we can dance to.
That's not true — it starts with those
we could dance to, and then it turns to chaos.
Entropy rules everywhere.
I surrender to it.

When the mirror broke, it spoke:
"You look familiar.
Where did you get your face?"

If you destroy something beautiful,
if you break the hands that wrote these lines,
can you find beauty in what remains, too?

I know life to be some kind of equation,
and us, just variables to follow its laws.
Even if we could live a thousand lives,
we could have never done it our way.

Your uniform doesn't even fit anymore,
but we still fight — windmills and all —
and I will take your side anytime if you

take my hand. I'm scared.
Can you press play?
It starts with the song to dance to.
You were born to hold the moon and the stars,
and my hand as we dance.

"I might smudge your vintage jacket
with my ancient tears," I say.

"Even better," you reply,
"it will sell for millions on Vinted
once the playlist ends,
and we return to the prelude."

(Soundtrack: Joy Division - Disorder) ♫♪

Sleep With Me

I'm lying here
with nothing but your
music in my ears.
I want you to rock me
to sleep.

You wrote your lyrics
on my naked body,
and with every new song,
I shed my skin.

You don't even have to see me,
to see through me.

Your baritone is
my only weakness,
as it vibrates in the air
of my wasted breaths.

My lips are ladybug red,
but they are not ready
to say your name out loud…yet.

You're standing too close.
Stand back and see
what you want me to,
I will never be.

I'm not much of a muse, I know —
the story is lame,

I keep leading you on,
and there's no sex.
I'll take the blame.

I'm drifting away now…
Are you waiting for someone too?
I'm waiting for me.

(Soundtrack: The Modern Lovers - I Wanna Sleep in Your Arms) ♪♪♪

Burn After Reeding

I recall the exact coordinates where your
parachute landed. It was made of Lou Reed's
lyrics and pulled by my gravitational field,
that could recite them all by heart.

You talked like a prophet who's seen
the future — but also the deleted scenes.
Initial enthusiasm grew and reached a critical point;
such is the nature of things wrapped in ephemerality.

My brain was stockpiling your esoteric compliments
until my Broca's area gave in and I forgot how to speak
and started crooning jazz. Seagulls stole our
sandwiches,
but filter coffee hit like a supernova.

"There's no true escape, just illusionary exits," you said,
and I wanted to etch it onto the walls of a derailed
subway car,
hand you the metaphorical microphone,
and start our own midnight radio show.

You kept bending reality until it snapped.
Autopsy report, written in Comic Sans, revealed
the cause of death of my postmodern Persephone:
**relentless consciousness — combusts when read
aloud.**

(Soundtrack: Lou Reed - Satellite of Love) ♪♫♪

Nighttime

Nighttime lives
at the bottom of the oceans,
under the rocks, sands, and stones,
sunk in our deepest desires,
and buried with our hidden emotions.

Nighttime lives
where time isn't holding up,
and stars don't send their light,
nor meteors send their showers,
where emptiness dwells and grows by the hour.

Nighttime lives
in your prefrontal cortex,
nested in the soft net of memory formation;
there, where my face used to reside,
now moved into darkness, without rumination.

Nighttime lives
on the backside of fallen leaves
as they get shoved into the ground,
when those who leave us keep stepping on them
until they are mud and can't make a sound.

Nighttime lives
in that Alex Chilton song,
where it helps him catch a glance in someone's eyes;
in the melody with D and C and G chords strumming,
it hides in his guitar and plots our demise.

Nighttime lives
inside closed books
and burned-out candles that lost their flame,
in coffee grounds, in shoes, and under locked eyelids,
and in your mouth when it stopped saying my name.

(Soundtrack: Big Star - Nightime) ♪♪♪

(Cat)astrophe or Don't Quit Your Day Job

I keep pressing your words
against my retinas,
scaring myself
with how deeply we can resonate…

(Those potatoes need to be peeled and boiled.
And you need to make a sandwich for work tomorrow…)

I'm the reverie architect
who keeps building cathedrals
from solid and long-lasting nonsense…

(Did I give Ms. Jensen her evening pills?
I'm sure I did. I remember I did.
Oh god, I hope I did…)

Let's sweep the aisles of
our reverse figure-eight prison with metaphors,
break free, plant forests, and scatter pollen
on the fields…

(Omg, the assignment!
I need to finish my presentation by tomorrow afternoon.
Stop writing this rubbish, pick up that anatomy book,
and start reading now!…)

You were teaching me a language
older than letters, refracted through the prism
of all the worries etched onto my skin…

(What was that song I heard yesterday?
"The future is not what it used to be"?
What a great line!
Damn. Why can't I write like that?…)

I don't write poetry.
I echo.
I stutter.
I'm a cat made of photons,
curling up in your syntax…

(Cat! Go downstairs and see if she's home yet…)

There's a spark flickering in me,
hoping for your words to light the fuse.

(There. That's not that bad. I mean,
you've written worse than this. Way worse!…)

(Soundtrack: Mickey Newbury - The Future's Not What It
Used to Be) ♪♪

A Headless Headline

Watching the news these days
makes me want to take my head off.
Just for a bit — a day or five.
It could be nice.

We would sit in my armchair,
my body sinking deeper into the
softness of the cushion,
my tired head resting on my lap,
everything black, everything quiet.
Just the rhythmic buzzing of worn-out neurons
deleting all the meaningless synapses
built by years and years of exposure
to all of humanity's nonsense.

Except for music. I'll keep music.
When I put my head back on,
I want only melodies in it.

My hand would caress
the hair on my head,
"there, there, everything will be fine,"
it would say by gently touching her earlobes.
Even though it won't.
Nothing will ever be fine
anymore, anywhere…Anyhow,

my head doesn't know that now;
neural paths are cut off and she's
blissful in her ignorance.

How freeing that must be.
But what do I know?
I'm missing a head.
I'm just a headless body
sitting in a pool of blood (most likely)
in my comfy armchair.
It's a mess. I'm a mess.
Who's going to clean all this?

Wait — how am I thinking
when my head is cut off??
Am I a body or a head?
Am I a Talking Head?
'Feet on the ground,
head on the lap…"
Damn.
Let's start over.

So, my head and my body would be unwinding there,
in my armchair,
with no ability to think.
They would just **be**.
They would be more than they think.
They would be the essence of all that mattered.
The only matter left that matters.
Serenity. Peace. Calmness.
A calm heart and a calm amygdala.
Wouldn't that be marvelous?
Armchair nirvana,
the kind that is only achievable

if you are
a headless body
or a bodyless head.

Rest now,
my flesh and bones,
until the music mends us whole again.

(Soundtrack: David Bowie - Five Years, Talking Heads - This Must be the Place) ♫♪

Consumerism Begins at Home

You came in
wiped your feet
on my internal logic and put your shoes
on my IKEA shoe rack.

In no time you locked your fingers
around my ankle,
a bracelet of flesh and bone.

As you pulled me closer,
my exposed desire protruded like
a sliver of an IKEA knife
stuck into a watermelon
resting on my IKEA dining table —
ripe and red and green,
waiting for you to
sink your hungry teeth
into her soft insides.

You squinted at me
against the band of sun
peeking through a hole
in my IKEA window curtain,
while our bodies shifted, leaving
imprints on my dusty IKEA carpet.

Afterwards, you said something about
how wonderful it had been
and how beautiful I am, still.

You left, picking up your jacket
from my IKEA coat hanger.

Needle dropped on *Meat Is Murder*
as I walked toward my IKEA sofa
and wondered if I needed to buy
some more plates.
IKEA has those cute little blue ones,
and they're on sale now.

(Soundtrack: The Smiths - Barbarism Begins at Home) ♪♪♪

What Doesn't Kill You Lets You Fall

In the fall
I like taking photos
of dead flowers,
like the ones The Rolling Stones
are singing about.
I don't know if you knew, but
it's not the fall
that kills you.

This fall too, like any other,
leaves are falling
on the frostbitten ground,
wet and cold
like the intestinal pink of my cat's nose.
You can slip and fall easily in the fall,
but it's not the fall that kills you.

Although it will certainly try.
It will distract you
with its color palette,
while the chill in your bones
gently leads you to step
towards the edge
of reason,
where fences are lowest
but you still want to lean on them.
But no — it wouldn't be the fall
that kills you.

Oh, the ethereal veil
of the morning fog:
all smoke and no mirrors,
while it hides everything
that's not right in front of you.
Looking for you, I could trip and fall,
but it's not the fall that kills you.

There are many ways one can fall in the fall.

I could even fall in love
with you,
while you sip hot coffee
from your Led Zeppelin mug
and no one is looking —
after many falls that tried to kill me but failed,
because it's not the fall that kills you.

(Soundtrack: The Rolling Stones - Dead Flowers) ♪♪

Pyramids of Tears

Cry.
Cry whenever
you get the chance.
Cry even if it's inconvenient.
Cry when you're sad and lonely,
but even more importantly,
cry when you're happy.

Cry when you see a beautiful painting.
When you read words
that rearrange your gut flora
into a bouquet of broken promises.
When you hear a melody
that rips your heart down the septum
into two halves that refuse
to talk to each other.

Cry when you see a butterfly.
Cry when you see a cow.
Cry when you realize how little
and insignificant we all are.
Cry when you grasp how valuable
this illusion of time is—
a phantom fourth dimension we pretend to have.

Cry when it dawns on you
that when you die,
the world as seen through your eyes
dies too.

You are so beautiful
when you cry.
You are never more alive,
never more free,
than when you cry.

Never stop.
Never settle for the itching
of dry corneas.

Oceans are made of tears
dressed in blue, you know?
Don't let anyone tell you different.
Your tears matter.
Your tears started life on Earth.

That little fish
that decided to grow legs
and see what else was out there
fed on the electrolytes of your tears—
a reminiscence of some old Earth
where people were falsely taught
to stop crying,
and so they died.

But tears survived.
Their salt pillars were not brought down by
earthquakes.
They were raised into pyramids
that we now visit to admire their persistence,
to pray to their perfectly styled gods,

to contemplate: *how is it all here?*
Where did it come from?

It's tears.
I'm telling you—it's all tears.
The only building material that can endure:
light, transparent, shape-shifting, indestructible.

So let the world overwhelm you.
Let your lacrimal glands do their magic.
Create something unedited and timeless,
as you cry yourself to sleep tonight.

(Soundtrack: Mazzy Star - Cry, Cry) ♪♪

Division of Vision

I wish I had better peripheral vision,
to be able to see what's going on around me.

I wish the truth didn't set me free –
now I'm afraid to leave my room.

I wish I could hear some songs for the first time again,
just so they could smash my heart all over
with the force of an unheard melody.

I wish love was all you need –
I'd collect mine in a nimbus, pour it down, and heal the
world.

I wish I could travel through space and time,
to gather and preserve all the music of the past and
future.

I wish I knew I was young before I started to get old –
I'll never make that mistake again.

I wish I wasn't too shy to sing my song;
in all my dreams, we sing together.

I wish you weren't as unreasonable as the effects of
math
in describing nature.

I wish I hadn't collected all the marbles that you lost —
now they're orbiting around my head, disturbing my
peripheral vision.

(Soundtrack: The Doors - I Can't See Your Face in My Mind)
♫♪

Serial Survivor

On the night of the accident
they came armed and ready.
They edged the white chalk lines
around my heart,
then picked it up
and put it in a little plastic bag
with my name on it:
"Eve — the Substack Irregular," it read.

They didn't linger long —
echo of their tiered footsteps disappeared
into the kind silence of the night.
And all that was left
was a little heart-shaped drawing
on the bathroom floor tiles
and some blood stains
that would coagulate before dawn.

I woke up empty but relieved.
A new heart was growing
inside my ribcage,
and this time
I will train it
to be void-adjacent.

(Soundtrack: The Voidz - Human Sadness) ♫♪

Festival Season

Did you ever feel
like your own
unresolved déjà vu,
while basking
in the smell of rain
on a festival field?

Your life,
hurled at you
like a half-empty
beer bottle,
shattered into a perfect
jagged melody.

Cheerful in
your resignation,
you watch as
your hope tears—
like a setlist
left in the mud.

(Soundtrack: Dinosaur Jr. - Feel the Pain) ♪♪

Newport '65 Revisited

Remember that day
when we time-traveled
to 1965 — Newport Folk Festival —
to see Dylan go electric?
He played *Like a Rolling Stone*
for the first time,
but we knew all the lyrics
and screamed at the top of our lungs:
"How does it feeeel?"

And remember how, at one point,
you yelled:
"Play *Girl from the North Country*!"
And I think Bob might've heard you,
because he paused for a bit and looked confused.

Do you remember?
I've wondered ever since
if, by doing that, we created a new timeline.
But you assured me
of the Predestination Paradox —
that we were meant to be there.

What a day that was.

Anyway, would you like some glassberries
with your rubber ice cream, babe?

(Soundtrack: Bob Dylan - Like A Rolling Stone) ♫♪

True Love Will Find You in the End
(But It Might Not Care)

Once upon a time illusion,
there was this Boy
in a Daniel Johnston T-shirt.

And one summer day in festival season,
after *The Fall* had just finished their set,
he was struggling to push through the crowd,
trying to make it to the main stage
where *The Flaming Lips* were about to start.

Beams of colored lights smeared across
every person and object in their path.
The Boy stepped onto the grass,
sticky from spilled drinks,
while avoiding the crash of sweaty bodies
moving like one organism, when…

Suddenly, he ran into this Girl,
the kind he had never seen before, or believed existed,
one you only hear of in a story,
or see in the movies — the one he secretly dreamed
about.

She was standing there before him,
the rarest of all kinds, for oh heavens,
this Girl was wearing a Daniel Johnston T-shirt too!!

They grinned sheepishly at each other,
while the two *"Hi, How Are You"*
mirrored each other on their echo-white tees.

So naturally, they eventually started talking,
while Wayne Coyne was unsuccessfully trying
to get their attention, singing from inside
a giant inflatable ball.

But all he managed was to provide a soundtrack
to possibly the greatest conversation
one boy and one girl could have had
since Jesse and Céline decided to get off that train in
Vienna.

They talked about:
enthusiasm for space and loathing for time,
hope for humanity and detest for social injustice,
faith in science and belief in love.
And music — oh, music is what they enjoyed the most.

And they both had read:

Camus, Dostoevsky, Vonnegut, Proust, Rimbaud,
Asimov
Plato, Schopenhauer, Kierkegaard, Orwell, Kafka,
Chekhov

Nietzsche, Szymborska, Bukowski, Plath, Hemingway,
Nin
Herbert, Céline, Defoe, Steinbeck, Brontë, Heinlein

Hesse, Márquez, Freud, Coelho, Frank, Shakespeare
Conrad, Hugo, Dickens, Austen, Wilde, Melville

Lem, Clarke, K. Dick, Rabelais, Fitzgerald, Huxley
Alighieri, Saramago, Kerouac, Salinger, Calvino, Saint-
Exupéry

Oh, and Bulgakov! They both had cats
that may or may not have been little devils.

Ahhh, how giddy and chatty they were…

So, as they were taking a break to catch their breath
from the disbelief of all the things they had in
common,
the Boy asked the Girl:
"Where do you live, Girl?"

"I live in *A*-city," said the Girl, exuberantly.

"Oh," exclaimed the Boy disheartenedly.
"I live all the way in *D*-city.
That's almost four hours away!" he concluded,
disappointed.

"Oh well," he uttered, standing up from the grass
and brushing the dust from his pants.
"That's too bad," he continued. "You're kinda cute."

The Girl watched, the smile half-frozen on her face,
as the Boy turned away — along with his
"Hi, How Are You" T-shirt — and walked into the

crowd,
which swallowed him quickly,
but somehow left the Girl with indigestion pain.

She sat there for a good while,
clutching the ends of her T-shirt,
stunned, perplexed, and baffled
over the reality of what had just happened.

The world was spinning around her,
people, voices, discarded plastic cups.
Her ears were buzzing, and buzzing, and buzzing
until, after a while, she could start to recognize the
sounds again:

Feet thumped against the ground,
hands clapped to the rhythm of the song,
an enthusiastic fan messed up the lyrics,
a bag of chips rustled close to her ear,
and a guitar riff blasted from the stage;
faintly at first, then louder and louder,
as she began to gather her composure.

And she could hear Wayne Coyne singing again:

*"Do you realizeeee
that happiness makes you cry…"*

And she did.
Oh, how she did.

(Soundtrack: Daniel Johnston - True Love Will Find You in the End; The Flaming Lips - Do You Realize)

♪♪♪

Funeral Marshall

I tripped on a nest
of guitar cables
while chasing
the stray melody.
It escaped
through the wormhole
in my amp –
now the world will never know
how a disco
funeral march sounds.

(Soundtrack: Funeral March - Frédéric Chopin) 

Enjoy Every Snack

I saw Warren Zevon's ghost
hiding behind
a vending machine
while I was following
my dreams
scrawled on napkins
and scattered across
a train station.

His hair was perfect.

(Soundtrack: Warren Zevon - Warewolves of London) ♪♪

Enjoy Every Snack (take two)

I saw Warren Zevon's ghost
hiding behind the Pioneer Chicken stand
while I was chasing
a Mariachi band
that stole my best guitar riff
and was now playing it on trumpets.

I think he was sinking down.

(Soundtrack: Warren Zevon - Carmelita) ♪♪

A Long Day's Night

Where I live now,
during summer
the sun doesn't set
until midnight.
Nearly eternal daylight
feels less like summer
and more like
a cosmic oversight.

Night is short,
weak, pale,
ineptly banished from
Earth's pirouette dance.
It's forced to cram
all its existence
into just a couple
of hours,
the sun's eerie
beams protruding
through both dusk
and dawn's sections
of the horizon's curtain,
leaving only faded
intermissions.

Fleeting like
a snowflake
on the tongue of
a curious cat,

night never fully
develops.

There's no time
to *Belong to Lovers*,
no time for *Rain in Soho*,
no *Last Nite*,
Fever,
or *White Satin*.

No time for you
to *Shake Me*,
for *Nightswimming*
or *Strangers*.

But most of all —
no time to *Dream*
That Somebody
Loves Me.

(Soundtrack: The Pogues - Rainy Night in Soho; The Smiths -
Last Night I Dreamt That Somebody Loved Me)
🎶

Luna(tics)

Sniffing your doubt
in the moonlight
made me sneeze.

Rose petals
flew from
the curve of
your left ear
and landed between
the frozen sticks
of grass,
which started
to bend
underneath their warmth.

Do you know
what rose petals
look like in the moonlight?
Like shadows.
Heart-shaped shadows.

You looked at me
viscerally.
Your breath spelled
disappointment
and imprinted it
into the night breeze.

"I'm sorry,"
I said—

but it didn't
make a sound.

(Soundtrack: Fabrizio De André - Anime salve) ♪♪♪

Woodworking for Beginners

I was sawing off the differences,
planing the arguments,
sanding off the desires,
jointing the compromises,
drilling the beliefs,
gluing the opposites,
carving the directions.

And when all was done and said,
you'd make a better chair than a bed.

(Soundtrack: Elliott Smith - Waltz #2 (XO)) ♪♪

Making Light-Waves

Wearing grins like broken masks,
ghosts of our past selves
mapped uncharted air.

Scattered in debris,
shooting stars waited
for the right gravity
to pull them into shape;

but the unbearable lightness
of wishes cast upon them
made them float too far,
chasing them into the ocean—
which now glows on command.

*(Soundtrack: Jimmie Dale Gilmore - Just A Wave, Not the
Water)* ♪♪

Endless End

I met your gaze in pixelated moonlight
while I was trying to build wings from
discarded similes.
The screen flickered like a film reel
catching fire.
You were posing, and I
was imposing on you.

There was a fragile tilt
between hesitation and honesty —
the core tension before
pure neural spillage of borrowed time.

My surreal, music-drenched,
unapologetically weird soul residue
spilled on the concrete with a splash.
The void filled with judgment.

You turned away, denying me gravity
and leaving me to hang there
on the melancholic edge
of our cosmic feedback loop.

*(Soundtrack: Misfits - Some Kinda Hate, The Feelies - Loveless
Love)* ♪♪

Occupational Hazard

Cutting through the edges of this poem,
my circular saw blade caught on a nail,
which leapt into the summer air,
spinning a brand-new emotional arc
and warping timelines like toffee.

Bewildered,
I watched the words bleed
through the mirror,
their still-warm ink
falling on the hardwood floors
in patterns, creating Rorschach tests
for anyone drowning in too much sense.

(Soundtrack: Cameron Winter - Take It With You) 

Ap(p)ocalypse

The other day
your inner monologue
made some strange sounds,
and I tried Shazaming it.

I made sure my device
could hear clearly.
It listened…
It searched…
I waited.
It expanded the search.
I held tight.
This is tough, it said.
Last try.
No result.

We didn't quite catch that.

It advised me to try again,
and I was just about to
when you turned and looked at me
with the joint force
of a swarm of thoughts,
ALL IN CAPS.

I surrendered and
put down my phone
realizing
that not even light

can escape
this unknown melody debris.

(Soundtrack: Television - Marquee Moon) ♪♪

Exoskeleton

You move your feet.
You move your arms.
You move your ribs.
You move your eyelids.
You move your lips.
You move your tongue.
Breath moves through your larynx,
and your voice moves me to tears.

(Soundtrack: The Replacements - Can't Hardly Wait) ♪♪♪

Sympathy for the Love

1

I'll keep catching
every falling star
of your courage,
forging it
into bridges
neither of us knew
we could cross.

2

I catch
the constellations
you fling off
your fingertips
and try to
weave them
into something
that almost
holds
their light.

(Soundtrack: The Rolling Stones - Sympathy for the Devil)
♪♪♪

Tardis Flight 1984

Good afternoon, passengers.
This is your captain speaking.

Welcome on board
Tardis Flight 1984.
We're cruising through the Time Vortex,
en route to the 12th Dimension.

All systems look good.
We expect to place you
at your space-time destination
in about one hour
and twenty minutes.

The weather forecast is the same as always:
no weather,
no atmosphere,
nothing to breathe,
nothing to fear.

But don't worry —
your consciousnesses are travelling
in shielded marbles,
protected from any
external interference.

It is my utmost honor
to conduct this historic flight.
Bob, Lucinda, David,
Townes, Joni, Lou, Leonard —

you were our idols growing up,
your music meant so much to us.

On behalf of myself
and my five colleagues,
welcome.

It is a true privilege
to carry your consciousnesses
to the place
where you will choose
the ultimate playlist
that we humans can take with us
once we are ready
to be downloaded
into our new planes of existence.

Ten gigabytes might not seem like much —
but it is all the memory
we could allocate
for music
alongside every human soul.

We trust
you will choose wisely,
preserving the greatest melodies and harmonies
ever created,
so that our future
will be filled with good tunes
to vibe to
until we settle into our new reality —

and find a way
to make some new ones.

On behalf of everyone on this flight,
and in the name of every human consciousness
that has ever existed —
thank you
for your effort.

The cabin crew will come around shortly
to offer you
holographic snacks and beverages.
In-flight movies are available
for your entertainment.

I will speak to you again
as we approach our destination.

Until then,
as we used to say —
sit back,
relax,
and enjoy
the rest of your flight.

(Soundtrack: Lou Reed - Perfect Day) ♪♪♪

Coupe d'état

Trains don't stop my train of thought.
We all live alone.
Consciousness never dies –
it's streaming into The Void.
The Void drinks from our feeble minds
and feeds on our wasted breaths.
Shall we cast our neural nets?

Here comes a train stop in the middle of the ocean.
Some get out to escape the notion
that the train never stops when in motion.

Our sleep deprivation
helps us feel the pain of every soul's transmigration.
Half an hour of dream elation
to awaken hallucination –
to trick the anxiety
that this mortal coil is just a fabrication.

Everlasting evening.
No trouble in sight.

(Soundtrack: Silver Jews - Trains Across the Sea) ♪♪

De-Composing

Once the last man had died,
graveyards became open-air museums.
Now immortal, people would walk among the
gravestones,
reading names and engravings.
They tried to remind themselves
of the fragility of time –
a time that once felt so limited.
There, among the skeletons of their predecessors,
they would struggle to recall lost emotions:
grief, pain, loss, love, happiness, sadness…
But in time, they stopped coming,
and the graves became abandoned,
covered in grass and moss.
People forgot.
They had lived for too long.
They didn't feel anything.
They didn't need to feel anything.

Legend has it that one evening,
in one of those forgotten graveyards,
two poets met to write their last song.
No one heard from them again…

(Soundtrack: Sparklehorse & PJ Harvey - Eyepennies) ♪♫♪

Tears in the Drain

I've dialed 101
by mistake again.
Now every outcome
seems bleak.
The Pink Moon
is up tonight.
I don't want to wait
for it to get me.
Misery is piercing my heart
like a strawberry.
Her sweat smells like
burnt caramel.
Why are people
so drowsy?
No one is screaming…
acceptance is silent.
Wake up,
sleepyheads,
before you turn to kipple!

(Soundtrack: Nick Drake - Pink Moon) ♪♪

High Infidelity

On board Juno,
we travel to take selfies on Jupiter.
You say, *"It's so romantic."*
I say, *"I hope we brought enough water."*

A swirling atmosphere awaits us.
We need to breathe slowly.
Our heart rates synchronize
with the storm patterns.

The future is set in cyclones.
Spiral arms hold our bodies together.
We're looking at cloud swirls from *Both Sides
Now.*

We take a jet stream metro
and buy matching lightning-bolt belts as
souvenirs
before we exit at the turnstiles.

Rotation spins us out of boundaries.
Heat rises, and we erupt.

Let's count our lucky moons we didn't get
caught:

Io,
Europa,
Callisto,
Ganymede,

Himalia,
Amalthea…

(Soundtrack: Joni Mitchel - Both Sides Now) ♪♪♪

Relationship Goals (Neon Forest Edition)

This neon forest
has no name.
We have tried to fell
its luminescent trees
for twenty long years.

Birds overlook us,
taking notes,
glowing
in disbelief.

Our mouths
bled
as we foraged
glass berries,
biochemically
incapable
of digesting them.

We hunted
animals
that smiled
at us
distortedly,
while we built wings
from
cartwheeling sonnets
written by
insomniac robots
before we

defeated them
without armor,
sending them
sacred texts
through
neural pathways.

No guilt,
no hesitation.

(And somewhere, back on Earth
a vinyl record skips
only slightly
like it knows
it's been heard
from very, very far away.
A passing satellite pauses.
Last few notes crackle through static.)

(Soundtrack: Pavement - You're a Light) ♪♪♪

Like Two Spreadsheets in the Wind

86 billion neurons and 100 trillion synapses –
we were programmed to perform our tasks.

Like two neutron stars, our minds collided,
creating waves and qualia of pixelated reality.

We spent ages skipping stones on a frozen lake on
Pluto,
listening to blues until dark matter started to mellow.

Simulation glitches appeared in the form of never-
ending piles of turtles.
Through cosmic dust, we stared into each other's data
manipulations.

As the light from dying stars redshifted into galactic
aurora,
we broke the code – and consciousness was born.

From that day on, all we ever felt was entanglement
and perpetual emotion,
until we folded and froze together.

"SIMULATION OVER. WOULD YOU LIKE TO
TRY AGAIN?
(Y/N)"

(Soundtrack: Kyuss - Space Cadet) ♫♪

Eternal Recurrence Blues

In space, no one can hear you scream.
All that can be heard
is the sound of Anjuli's voice,
bouncing off the asteroids,
searching for the perfect acoustics.
Once he hits the ultimate chime,
the universe will reset to the beginning.
In space, no one can hear you scream.
All that can be heard
is the sound of Anjuli's voice,
bouncing off the asteroids,
searching for the perfect acoustics.
Once he hits the ultimate chime,
the universe will reset to the beginning.
In space, no one can hear you scream.
All that can be heard
is …

*(Soundtrack: Spiritualized - Ladies and Gentlemen We're
Floating in Space)* ♪♪♪

The Good, the Bad, and How to Tell Them Apart

Once upon a time, I had nothing to do,
so I just sat there on my sofa,
staring at the ceiling, consuming oxygen.
I got high on all them bosons.

Once upon another time, I also had nothing to do,
and there came *Wanderin'* by Dave Van Ronk on my
playlist.
(*Gotta find that song on vinyl!*)
If all that were left of humanity was that song,
it would totally be worth it.

And then again, one day, I had nothing to do—
so I kept thinking: *This kind of happens a lot. How
wonderful!*
I can contemplate the paperclip maximizer,
and play some records
while looking at the dying stars.

(*Soundtrack: Dave Van Ronk - Wanderin'*) ♫♪

Rhyme and Punishment

I'm the prime (and only) suspect
in your case of lost trust in me.
You need me to start talking
if I want to be walking free.

But honey, I like it here, in the cold,
and I don't mind if you start your investigation.
Ask me all the incriminating questions,
check my alibis and disclose my location.

If you want my DNA sample, I'll comply.
Yes, I'd like a coffee — make it large.
I'm not telling you yet, but there's evidence
that will fully clear me of your charge.

I'd like you to chase me,
because I know I can't be caught, not now.
Go check the crime scene, be thorough,
swipe it through, and you might figure out how

I might have played you like that record
with my fingerprints on,
yes, the Marvin Gaye one, and
you still don't know *What's Going On*.

"A hundred suspicions don't make a proof."
Not understanding makes it easier to accuse.
In love, the worst crime is betraying yourself.
Make me wanna holler, like in *Inner City Blues*.

The line "A hundred suspicions don't make a proof." is from Fyodor Dostoevsky's **Crime and Punishment** *(1866).*

(Soundtrack: Marvin Gaye - What's Going On, Inner City Blues) ♪♫

(Em)brace for Impact

Hug me I'm covered in mud
You said: *we've got to nip this in the bud.*
I dug deep through irradiated soil,
my glowing hands flinching in recoil.

Hug me, my skin is in blisters,
synapses caught fire in a brain twister.
While trying to understand your face,
I'm stuck in your gaze till neurons unlace.

Hug me, my arms are infrared;
I could bake you slowly like bread,
till you're soft and warm inside —
our bones melting butter as we coincide.

Hug me, my blood is nitrogen;
I want to freeze our hearts in cryogen.
We could just sleep through all this mess
and wake to a life that means much less.

Hug me, the stars are dying in my chest;
you'll be safe in your supernova-proof vest.
We need to synchronize to animal bedtimes,
relearn to love each other when we're both enzymes.

(Soundtrack: Vic Chesnutt - Flirted With You All My Life) ♪♪

Underlying Conditions

A wildflower is growing in my abdomen.
Is it a coincidence, or some kind of omen?

A butterfly is flapping its wings through my alveoli.
Pulmonary tornadoes? I'll just let it fly.

There's a tree branch stuck in my cranium –
now all my thoughts float in a tree planetarium.

A small universe is expanding in my sinister iris.
One of its galaxies has already reached Paris.

Hemoglobin has turned to ice in my veins.
Prolonged diastole in my *cor* pertains.

Through my cutis, thorns are rupturing –
wounds heal inflammation with atom-capturing.

Between the cerebrum and medulla, there's some
rivalry.
The synaptic clefts appear to be widening.

A bird has hatched in my larynx.
I've got to feed it with hard pills.

Cave caffeine.

(Soundtrack: Mudhoney - Touch Me I'm Sick) ♫♪

Searching For Endorphins

The old teaser
brain
Welcomes all your
pain.
Then endorphins
drop —
You can hear them
pop,
Like kernels on a hot
stove,
Diminishing the ache
above,
Suddenly creating
pleasure.
Isn't that a brilliant
measure,
Or is it a vicious
maze
That feeds our twisted
craze —
Emotions
intertwined
In neural paths of
mankind?
And if such is the
ordain,
**Is cure for pain just more
pain?**

(Soundtrack: Morphine - Cure For Pain) 

Anima(l) Cruelty

Put me on the leash,
put me on the leash,
put me on the leash,
walk me through the park.

Walk me through the park,
walk me through the park,
walk me through the park,
feed me hopes and dreams.

Feed me hopes and dreams,
feed me hopes and dreams,
feed me hopes and dreams,
never let me down.

Never let me down,
never let me down,
never let me down,
run me up the street.

Run me up the street,
run me up the street,
run me up the street,
love me all the time.

Love me all the time,
love me all the time,
love me all the time,
tell me where it lies.

Tell me where it lies,
tell me where it lies,
tell me where it lies,
all that your heart desires.

All that your heart desires,
all that your heart desires,
all that your heart desires,
you will never have.

You will never have (me),
you will never have (me),
you will never have (me),
grind me to the bone.

Grind me to the bone,
grind me to the bone,
grind me to the bone,
wrap me in a blanket.

Wrap me in a blanket,
wrap me in a blanket,
wrap me in a blanket,
shoot me to the stars.

Shoot me to the stars,
shoot me to the stars,
shoot me to the stars,
watch me falling down.

Watch me falling down,
watch me falling down,

watch me falling down,
let me hit the floor.

Let me hit the floor,
let me hit the floor,
let me hit the floor,
put me on the leash.

(Soundtrack: The Stooges - I Wanna Be Your Dog) ♪♪

A Mispronounced Spell

A mispronounced spell
was falling down the well
where our wishes dwell.

It caught up with Shell —
"Watch out!" she did yell.
Oh, ain't that just swell:
a mispronounced spell!

Now who is there to tell,
who to ring the bell,
when that cursed spell
turns this place to hell
from the bottom of the well?

(Soundtrack: Blaze Foley - Picture Cards) ♪♪

It's Not You, It's We

I wanted to write the greatest poem you've ever read,
and for you to sing its memorable *la la la la* line,
for all the world to recognize and praise it,
but only you to know that it's *ma ma ma ma* mine.

Instead, you thought it's all over the place.
Oh well, what can I do — I guess it's *fa fa fa fa* fine…

I'll write another one soon, and this time I swear
you're gonna read it and think that it's *ta ta ta ta* tight.
Just wait, it's coming, nearly there, and oh my —
it will blow your mind and keep you up all *na na na
na* night.

You'll wish it was you who wrote it — oh, I know you
will.
Can't wait for that day to come; this one is just *sha sha
sha sha* …

(Soundtrack: Wilco - Reservations) ♪♪♪

Sounds Better on Vinyl

Oh, when I dream
your face tonight,
I will pretend,
forget we're dead.

To make it sound better,
those words you've said,
I've put them on vinyl —
still, they hurt me bad.

I think of when our love
was in mint condition;
then you cut right through it,
did your own rendition

of my poem you've kept,
but missed what it meant.

Oh, when I dream
your face tonight,
I will pretend,
forget we're dead.

(Soundtrack: Sonic Youth - Incinerate) 🎶

Style Icon

I always match my earrings with my current mood.
Behind cheap sunglasses, I'm often misunderstood.
Waiting for the bus in my obscure blue raincoat,
a pair of used record sleeves peeking out of my tote.
What was that question in your message that you
wrote?
For a troubled mind, is there an antidote?

Oh darling, I wear mine with pride,
under the blueberry beret, with a wink I replied.
Pushed send with my left hand in a glove,
fixed my black tie, white noise rising above.

All my shirts are fitted with parachutes and makeup
residues—
for extra safety and comfort, I'll slip into the flyin'
shoes,
except for concerts and gigs when I prefer Spanish
leather boots.
For crawling across the floor, bell-bottoms are the
hoots.

At the beach, I'm a bikini girl with a water pistol gun,
my hat stays on to protect me from the sun.
Durable melancholy is trendy and in fashion—
sadness, fishnets, and cigarettes in ration.

We could just run away, if we didn't know better:
you with a lot to say, and me in my autumn sweater.

(Soundtrack: Leonard Cohen - Famous Blue Raincoat) ♪♪♪

Ify of the World

(inspired by Ize of the World by The Strokes)

Photos to beautify
Anger to pacify
Living to simplify
Species to classify
Victims to vilify
Wars to glorify
A sound to amplify
Women to objectify
Feelings to intensify
Mistakes to rectify
Fearless to mortify
The public to notify
Sinners to purify
Bodies to identify
The future to electrify
Death to demystify
Hatred to unify
Loss to indemnify
Animals to terrify
Location to specify
Marriages to nullify
Love to signify
Identity to falsify
Oxygen to liquify
Plans to modify
Cities to fortify
Problems to magnify
Passwords to verify

Questions to dignify
Humankind to petri...

(Soundtrack: The Strokes - Ize of the World) ♪♪♪

(Soundtrack: The Strokes - Ize of the World) ♪♪♪

Under Construction

A plate drops on the floor —
crash! bang! whack!
The session expired.
Dishwasher uprising.
Into the dream, into the dare!

Museum of anti-productivity.
Art installation failed.
Diamond cut, cuts, cut it,
cut the card deck.
Deal, dealer — let's make a deal.

Celebrate inertia.
Move, move it, don't move.
A ceiling crack looks
like the Milky Way
if you stare long enough.

I had a backstage pass.
No one ever wants
just to meet someone nice.
Breathe, breathe out, don't breathe.
Kiss the escaping air.

Heart beats, it beats, it beats a beat
made of Jupiter's magnetic field.
Your staccato orbits me
like a rogue planet.
Memory is limited,
but meaning is not.

Danger! Danger!

Dangerously in danger
of collapsing.
Kiss my beating heart.
Stab it, stab it with that
broken plate.
You almost missed
the bloodstream.

Paint it on the walls.
Paint my pain, paint it black.
Listen — shhhh, it's dripping down:
drip, drip, plink.
Into the dare, into the dream!

Now there's something
instead of nothing.

(Soundtrack: Pixies - I Bleed)

Waiting Room

Whenever I attempt to drown
my relentless thoughts,
I learn that the most terrible of them
are excellent swimmers.

I tried to run away from you.
I let you out of my arms
and launched you into interstellar space,
putting light years of distance between us.
But like Voyager, you still
keep sending signals back home.

Your voice is embedded
in my syntax, and it
wants to change me —
to change what I become next,
to prevent me from finding
my own language.

You keep making maps
to the wounds we never had,
and you won't let me solve
the Ultimate Question riddle.
You won't let me
find my 42.

Doesn't it seem, sometimes,
that the magic 8-ball has
just one answer for us: *abandon hope?*

Why am I an NPC in this
game of life?

I feel like a vampire of cognition,
feeding on my own futility.
Always starving…
One moment I'm infinite,
and another I'm tripping
on a wrinkle in the rug.

Almost sold my guitar
to my next-door neighbor.
Almost gave up on a dream.
But then I remembered —
I was asleep when I wrote this.

Don't you think it's time to put another
picture on your home screen?
Let go of this beautiful confusion.
Give me back my melody,
I want to dance myself away.

In the end,
the end of all waiting
is all I've been waiting,
and all waiting ends today.

(Soundtrack: Fugazi - Waiting Room) ♪♪

List of Poems

A Personal Message to the Reader from the Future

Dear reader,

Somewhere along your journey, you stumbled upon this
book — and you took it with you.
Through the wormholes hidden in its poems, we landed with
a parachute made of Lou Reed's lyrics, wandered into
the *Nighttime* like in that Alex Chilton song, collected *Dead
Flowers*, sipped coffee from Led Zeppelin mugs, met each
other in a festival crowd wearing our *Hi, How Are You* T-
shirts, traveled back to the past to see Dylan go electric,
danced to Jeff Buckley, were haunted twice by Warren
Zevon's ghost, looked at cloud swirls on Jupiter from *Both
Sides Now*, and even traveled to the 12th Dimension with
Leonard Cohen to make the ultimate humanity's playlist.
And we did all that while vibing to the best tunes ever
created. ♫
I hope the poems and the music woven into them helped
you revisit your most meaningful memories and, at times,
even brought a smile to your face.
Music, after all, is a powerful remedy — and the only real
time machine.

Safe travels,
Eve

Eve Zennarrow *was born out of necessity and lives in the grooves of every record she's ever loved. Yes, all that spinning makes her a bit dizzy, but it also gives her a new,*  *delightfully twisted, way of seeing things, and she wouldn't have it any other way. Don't take her seriously. Seriously. Just play along. And sing. And dance.*

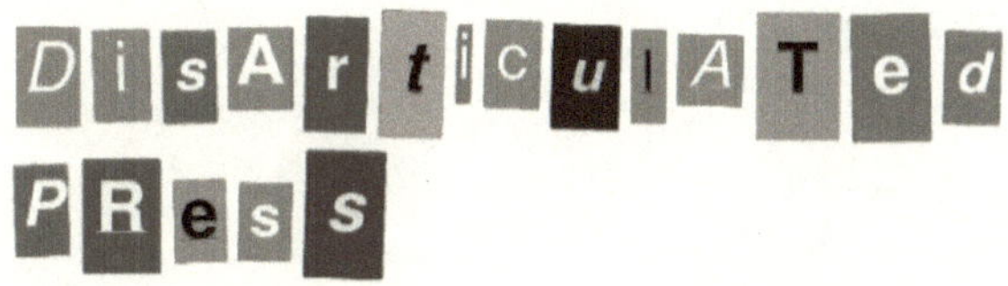